The Legend of the

by ALVIN TRESSELT *and* NANCY CLEAVER

Willow Plate

with pictures by JOSEPH LOW

Parents' Magazine Press, New York: 1968

No one knows who first told the story of the willow plate. We do know that the popular willow-pattern dinnerware was first manufactured in England around 1780 and that it is actually a combination of several designs often found on porcelain imported from China at that time. Ever since, the willow pattern has remained a household favorite, and today it is seen even on paper napkins and paper plates. Perhaps the legend originated in England. Or possibly it was some old Chinese storyteller, heeding the cries of a circle of children for "just one more story" who began spinning the tale of Chang and his love for the beautiful Koong-se. It is easy to find the places mentioned in the story on the plate. In the center is the palace of T'so Ling, shaded by a willow tree. At the lower left is the summer house where Koong-se spent her days, and in front of it is the bridge. You can even see the figures of Koong-se and Chang running away from the angry T'so Ling. Below is the fence the father built to keep away suitors. Above the willow is the boat that the two lovers escaped in, and beyond that is the island where they found happiness. Sad to say, the house on the island is already in flames but, high above, at the top of the plate, Koong-se and Chang fly as immortal doves, forever free.

In the land of China, during the reign
of the emperors, there lived a wealthy
mandarin named T'so Ling. His lands were
broad and fertile, and his treasures were
beyond counting. His palace was built
of fine woods and rich lacquers, with a roof
of tiles that gleamed in the sun. Beside it
ran a wide river, and a graceful willow
gave shade in the heat of the day.

But of all his possessions, the mandarin delighted
most in his daughter, Koong-se. Her beauty dazzled
all who looked upon her, and her heart was as
gentle as the birds who nested in the bamboo
thickets beside the river. Koong-se passed her days
in a summer house that leaned over the rippling
waters. Here she did fine embroidery on silk
from far-off Shantung while her faithful nurse,
Chun Soy, told tales of old China, and her little
bird sang sweetly in his cage of bamboo.

Now among the many people who worked for the

wealthy T'so Ling, there was a young clerk

named Chang whose greatest desire was to be a poet.

He had no sooner laid eyes on the beautiful

Koong-se when he fell in love with her.

She, too, was charmed by this handsome young

man, and she invited him to visit her in the

summer house so that he might read his poems

to her, while old Chun Soy kept watch.

Alas, one day as Chang was reading, the old nurse's eyes grew heavier and heavier until suddenly she was fast asleep. And the gods of China willed that at that very moment the mandarin should choose to visit his cherished Koong-se. Aiyie! Then how great was his anger when he discovered a humble clerk seated at his daughter's feet reading poetry!

"Pig! Son of Swine!" he cried. "How dare a peasant like you cast his gaze upon the daughter of a mandarin! Get out, and if I ever see you on my lands again I will have you cut up and fed to the crows!" And while Koong-se's heart broke with pity for Chang, the poor man fled from the wrath of her angry father.

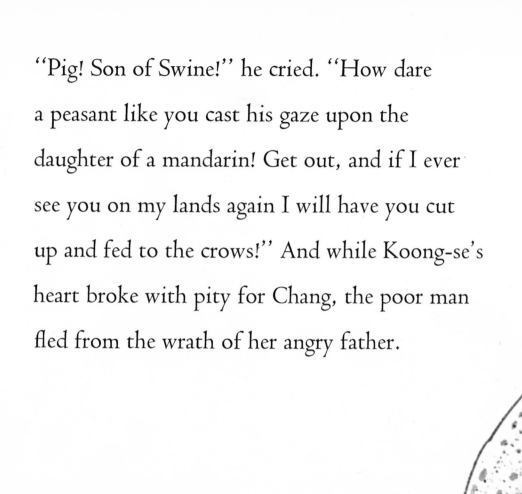

Of course the old nurse was dismissed at once, and a woman whose temper was as ugly as her face was put in charge of Koong-se. The mandarin shut up his daughter in a pavilion right outside his windows so that he could keep a close watch on her. He built a high fence about his palace so that no unwanted suitors could come near the heartbroken Koong-se.

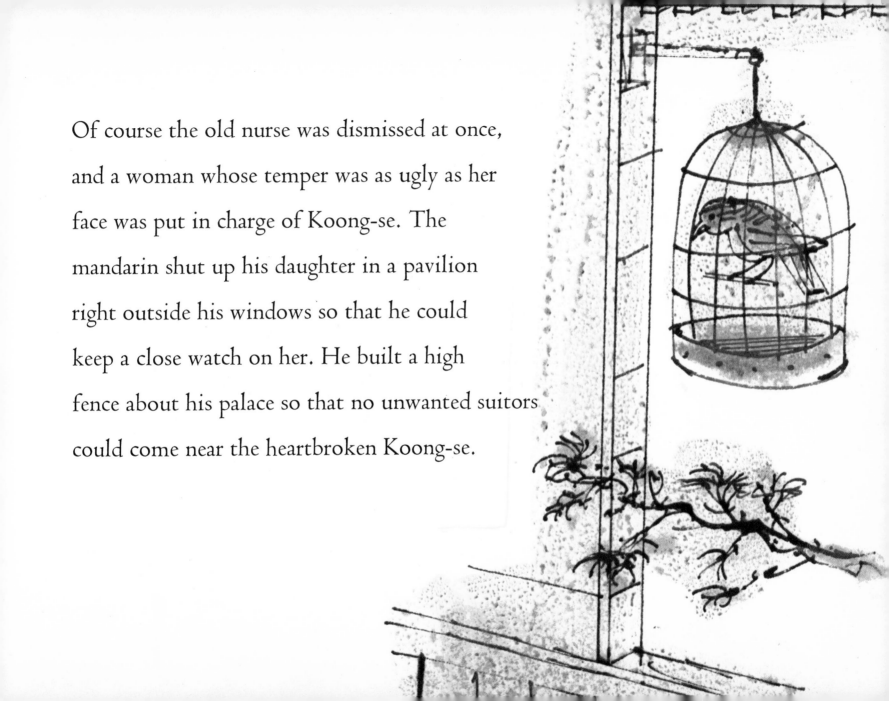

Now, as was the custom in the days of the emperors, T-so Ling set about to choose a husband for his daughter. He at length offered her hand to a rich and powerful mandarin named Ta-jin, and the marriage was set for the time of the blooming of the peach trees. Ta-jin was a mighty man, with many soldiers at his command, but his face was haughty and cruel.

Koong-se wept bitterly when she heard of her approaching marriage, but she was an obedient daughter and she never thought to disobey her father. Then one day as she sat in the pavilion beside the water, she spied a tiny boat fashioned out of a coconut shell.

The cross old nurse was nowhere near so she quickly pulled it from the river as it drifted under her window. Imagine her joy when she discovered it carried a note from Chang, telling her of his great love. Quickly she wrote explaining about her coming marriage and begging him to rescue her from the hateful mandarin. Then saying a prayer to Kwan-yin, the goddess of mercy, she set the little boat adrift once more.

Now the time of the blooming of the peach trees was near at hand. The day of the wedding was announced and the palace was alive with great activity. Daily, gifts of breathtaking beauty arrived at the gates . . . silken robes, carvings of rare white jade, great bronze incense burners, lacquered bowls and strange and wonderful birds in golden cages. But the most beautiful of all was a chest of jewels from Ta-jin for the delight of his new bride. Poor Koong-se's eyes were so red from weeping she could scarcely see the gifts, and their beauty gave no pleasure to her heart.

All too soon came the eve of the wedding.
T'so Ling had prepared a feast of celebration,
inviting noblemen and princes from the far
corners of China, and the splendor of the
company was great to see. Koong-se, as a mere
woman, was not permitted to take part in
the banquet, so as the men feasted, the
poor bride sat in her pavilion and wept.

But fortunately, Kwan-yin in her mercy had
heeded the prayers of the poor girl and she
had guided the coconut shell back to the
watching Chang. He disguised himself as
a guest of the mandarin and, what with the
great crowd attending the feast, it was not
difficult for him to walk unnoticed inside
the high fence about the palace. Chang
made sure to drink none of the many cups
of rice wine that passed among the guests.

Then as the party grew louder and more boisterous he slipped away to the pavilion where Koong-se sat. The nurse, feeling sure that the girl would be safe on a night such as this, had gone into the palace kitchen to gossip with the servants and to taste some of the rare foods that had been prepared for the banquet. In a twinkling Chang had his beloved in his arms.

But the gods do not always make things easy
for lovers, for just then the old nurse
waddled in to make sure Koong-se was all right.
Such a hue and cry she set up when she
discovered what had happened! Running into
the banquet hall she called upon the mandarin
to drive off the intruder. Without wasting
a minute Chang and Koong-se fled, but not
before she wisely thought to pick up the
chest of jewels Ta-jin had given her.

Off they ran across the bridge to the summer
house with the old mandarin close behind them.
But, the truth was that he had drunk too
many cups of rice wine, and besides, he had not run
so much as a step since his youth, so the
lovers were soon able to escape. Once in
the summer house they were hidden by the
faithful Chun Soy who had continued to
live there unbeknownst to the mandarin.

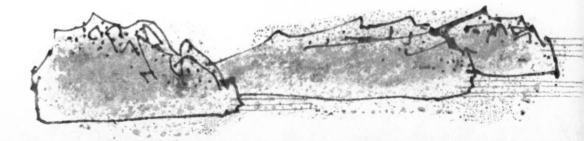

Not long were they safe, however, for soon

T'so Ling summoned his guards, and as they

marched on the summer house to capture them,

Chang and Koong-se were forced to flee

in a small boat down the broad river.

For many days and nights they drifted along until one night they moored their boat in the shelter of a small island. Finding it in a wild and uncultivated state, they determined to make it their own. With a few of the jewels from the casket they purchased the island, and with hard work and care they turned it into a place of beauty.

Their simple house was surrounded with gardens where they raised
all manner of vegetables to sell to the boatmen who passed on the river.
Soon the names of Chang the gardener and Koong-se his beautiful
wife were known up and down the length of the mighty river.

But, sad to say, this was their undoing. Ta-jin
had never forgotten the beauty of Koong-se, nor
could he easily put aside the fact that she
had been stolen from him by a poor peasant who
fancied himself a poet. Therefore, he had
spies in the countryside whom he paid to
bring him word, should they ever learn of the
whereabouts of the two lovers. And so it was
that one day Ta-jin was told that Chang and
Koong-se were living happily on the island.

He gathered round him a group of his soldiers
and they sailed down the river to the island.
Rushing up from the shore they surprised Chang
working in the gardens. The poor man fought
bravely, but with only a gardener's hoe
to defend himself he was soon overcome.
Koong-se, coming to a window to learn what
the excitement was all about, saw with
horror the death of her beloved Chang.

Having finished with him, the soldiers turned to the house so that they might capture Koong-se. But the poor girl, recognizing Ta-jin as the leader, rushed about, closing all the doors and windows. Then without hesitation she set fire to the house and perished in the flames.

Now, indeed, was the heart of the goddess Kwan-yin touched with pity, and bending down from her throne in the heavens she touched Chang and Koong-se. Instantly they were turned into doves. And from that day on they flew free and happy, high in the blue skies of China.